Padma
the Pirate
Fairy

Join the **Rainbow Magic Reading Challenge!**

Read the story and collect your fairy points to climb the
Re~~ading Rainbow at the back of the book~~

To Maisie Joan, who loves the fairies

Special thanks to
Rachel Elliot

ORCHARD BOOKS

First published in Great Britain in 2020 by The Watts Publishing Group

1 3 5 7 9 10 8 6 4 2

© 2020 Rainbow Magic Limited.
© 2020 HIT Entertainment Limited.
Illustrations © Orchard Books 2020

A CIP catalogue record for this book is available from the British Library.

ISBN 978 1 40835 244 1

Printed and bound in Great Britain by Clays Ltd, Elcograf S.p.A

The paper and board used in this book are made from wood from responsible sources

Orchard Books
An imprint of Hachette Children's Group
Part of The Watts Publishing Group Limited
Carmelite House, 50 Victoria Embankment, London EC4Y 0DZ

An Hachette UK Company
www.hachette.co.uk
www.hachettechildrens.co.uk

Padma
the Pirate
Fairy

By Daisy Meadows

ORCHARD

www.rainbowmagicbooks.co.uk

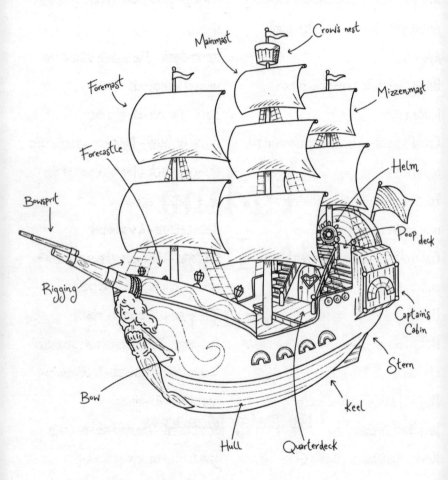

Pirate Glossary

Aft - Towards the back of the ship

Ahoy - A call to get someone's attention

Avast ye! - Stop and pay attention!

Aye - Yes

Bilge - Silly talk, or the lowest part inside a ship

Crow's nest - A lookout platform at the top of a mast

Forecastle - The part of the deck nearest the front of a ship

Gangplank - A ramp between a ship and dry land

Helm - A ship's steering wheel

Hold - The storage area in the lower part of a ship

Hull - The main body of a ship

Jack Tar - A sailor

Keel - The underneath of a ship

Landlubber - Someone who isn't used to life at sea

Mainmast - The longest mast

Mizzenmast - The largest mast

Parley - A discussion between opposite sides

Poop deck - The highest deck at the stern of a large ship

Port - The left side of a ship

Prow or bow - The front part of a ship

Quarterdeck - The back part of the upper deck of a ship

Rapscallion - A scoundrel

Rigging - The ropes, chains and tackle used to control masts and sails.

Scallywag - A mischief-maker

Sea legs - The ability to walk on a ship

Shiver me timbers! - Goodness me!

Spyglass - A telescope

Starboard - The right side of a ship

Stern - The back part of a ship

Swashbuckler - Adventurous swordsman

Ye - You

Contents

Story One:

The Bejewelled Treasure Chest

Chapter One: Briny-on-Sea	11
Chapter Two: The Rainbow Pearl	21
Chapter Three: Captain Frostbeard	29
Chapter Four: Cannon-Fire	39
Chapter Five: The Pirate Code	49

Story Two:
The Swashbuckling Pirate Hat

Chapter Six: Goblin on the Galleon   61
Chapter Seven: Risky Rigging   71
Chapter Eight: A Right Royal Disaster   79
Chapter Nine: Wingless   89
Chapter Ten: Winged Pirates   99

Story Three:
The Jolly Parrot

Chapter Eleven: Silly Shanties   111
Chapter Twelve: Goblins and Mermaids   119
Chapter Thirteen: Jack Frost's Plan   127
Chapter Fourteen: Seals and Dolphins   135
Chapter Fifteen: Shimmer and Shake   143

Frostbeard's Shanty

Shiver me timbers and yo ho ho!
This prattling fairy has to go.
Frostbeard the Fearsome will never rest
Until he possesses her treasure chest.

Leave the castle cold and dank,
And make that fairy walk the plank.
Avast ye, goblins! Make her flee.
The Rainbow Pearl belongs to me!

Story One
The Bejewelled
Treasure Chest

Chapter One
Briny-on-Sea

"Just taste the salt in the air," said Rachel
Walker, holding on to the ship's rail. "I
love being at sea."

She put her head back and the warm
breeze blew back her hair. Her best
friend, Kirsty Tate, leaned forward over
the railings, watching the ship's prow

plunge through the water.

"I never thought I'd be standing on a real pirate ship," she said. "What's the name of this front part of the deck?"

"The forecastle," Rachel reminded her.

"Oh, yes, I remember," Kirsty replied. "And the high deck at the back of the ship is called the poop deck, and everything in between is the quarterdeck, right? Hey, I think I'm getting the hang of being a pirate."

"You forgot the main deck and the gun deck," said Rachel. "And then there's the mizzenmast and the mainmast and the foremast . . . but I can't remember which one is which."

"I think that means we're still landlubbers," said Kirsty with a laugh.

The ship was called the *Golden Galleon*,

and it belonged to her dad's friend Jake. He had invited the Tate family on a sailing trip to Briny-on-Sea, which held the biggest pirate festival of the year. Best of all, Kirsty had been allowed to bring her best friend along.

"What exactly is Jake's job?" Rachel asked. "He's not a real pirate, is he?"

"He does pirate birthday parties on the ship, and he performs a show at all the pirate festivals," said Kirsty. "Oh, I think I hear him coming."

Hearing heavy footsteps behind them, they turned around and saw Jake with Mr Tate.

"You really do look magnificent," Mr Tate was saying.

Jake grinned. He was already wearing his pirate outfit: buckled boots, a red-and-gold tailcoat and a three-cornered hat.

"Briny-on-Sea has the biggest pirate festival of the year," he said. "You're all in for a swashbuckling time, me hearties."

"What sort of things happen at a pirate festival?" Rachel asked.

"There will be music and singing," said Jake. "Lots of face-painting, cannons and sword-fighting demonstrations, and amazing street food on every corner, of course. My favourite part is the pirate parade on the last day of the festival. All the pirates from the festival march through the town, singing shanties and waving their cutlasses."

Jake showed them the pin badges on his hat, each one from a different country. He told them lots of stories about pirate festivals around the world. It seemed no time at all before the *Golden Galleon* was moored in Briny-on-Sea's harbour.

Tea was a feast fit for a pirate king, served on a polished wooden table as the sun was setting. After pudding, Rachel and Kirsty were allowed to sit

up on deck and watch the stars come out. Each of them was wrapped in a blanket, holding a tankard of warm, spiced blackcurrant drink. Gurgling water lapped against the sides of the ship.

"Briny-on-Sea looks peaceful,"

said Rachel, gazing at the little lights twinkling across the town.

"It won't be that peaceful tomorrow, by the sound of it," said Rachel. "I can't wait."

Kirsty looked up at the starry sky and gasped.

"What is it?" asked Rachel.

"Something just passed in front of the moon," Kirsty said in a breathless voice. "It looked like a pirate ship!"

19

Chapter Two
The Rainbow Pearl

"There it is," said Rachel.

A glittering shape was leaving a sparkling trail across the evening sky.

"It's too big to be a shooting star," said Kirsty. "And it can't be a ship."

But it was! Luckily, Rachel and Kirsty had seen plenty of magic before, so they weren't scared. The ship came closer, and the girls saw a smiling mermaid carved into its wooden prow.

"The portholes are shaped like rainbows," Kirsty said, jumping to her feet.

The ship was now close enough for them to read its name, inlaid in gold: *Rainbow Pearl*.

"It's a fairy ship," said Rachel, tingling with happiness.

A fairy was waving to them from the rigging. The girls waved back at her. She had long, brown curls that tumbled down her back, and was wearing a green jacket with gold buttons and fitted black trousers, with a wide belt buckled loosely around her hips.

"Ahoy there!" she called. "I'm Padma

the Pirate Fairy."

"Hello, Padma," said Kirsty. "It's lovely to meet you."

"We didn't know that there would be fairies at the festival," said Rachel.

The *Rainbow Pearl* sailed down and landed on the deck beside the girls. Padma fluttered up and hovered in front of them.

"It's my job to watch over pirates," she said. "Queen Titania told me that you were both here. I couldn't wait to meet you."

"What are you going to be doing while you are here?" Kirsty asked.

"I'll be busy keeping pirates and visitors safe and happy," said Padma. "Luckily, I have three magical objects that give me all the magic I need to do my job."

"What are they?" asked Rachel.

Padma smiled.

"The bejewelled treasure chest protects pirates' most precious objects," she said. "The swashbuckling pirate hat protects

pirates from injury. And the jolly
parrot helps people on board ship to
communicate well."

"Do you travel everywhere in your
ship?" Kirsty asked.

Padma gave them a beaming smile.
"Yes, isn't she wonderful?"

"She?" said Rachel. "Is your ship a girl?"

"It's a tradition that all ships are called 'she'," Padma explained. "I feel as if the *Rainbow Pearl* is a friend who shares my adventures. We've had so much fun together."

Just then, they heard Mr Tate's voice calling from below decks. "Girls, it's time for bed."

Padma fluttered back on to her ship, and the *Rainbow Pearl* began to rise into the sky again.

"Good night," Padma called. "I'll come and find you tomorrow."

The girls waved, and then hurried down the steep ship's ladder to their cabin. There were two hammocks hanging side by side. Each one had its

own mattress, a squashy pillow and a thick quilt. A glowing lantern hung from the ceiling, swinging gently as the ship rocked. Rachel and Kirsty were asleep as soon as their heads touched the pillows.

Chapter Three
Captain Frostbeard

Rachel and Kirsty woke to the shrill cries of seagulls. Sunshine streamed through the tiny cabin windows. Rachel slipped out of her hammock and peeped outside.

"Oh, a new ship arrived in the night," she said. "It's moored next to us."

Kirsty came to look.

"It's an old one," she said. "Look, it has
a mermaid on the prow, like the *Rainbow
Pearl*."

Rachel grabbed her friend's arm.

"It has rainbow portholes too," she said.
"That's odd."

Kirsty gasped.

"Look at the name," she said. "It *is* the *Rainbow Pearl*!"

"Maybe Padma made it human size so we could explore it," said Rachel. "Come on, let's go up on deck and get a better look."

They pulled on their clothes and raced up to the main deck. The *Rainbow Pearl* looked even more magnificent now that they could see the whole ship.

"It's even bigger than the *Golden Galleon*," said Kirsty. "How funny . . . it has a sort of blue glow."

"It must be a trick of the light," said Rachel.

"But where is Padma?" Kirsty went on. "And where did all the crew come from?"

The pirate crew were wearing green-and-white striped trousers, white shirts

31

and green waistcoats. Bandanas were
tied around their heads, and their big
black boots made a great din on the
wooden deck.

"They've all got the same straggly hair," said Rachel. "Do you think they're wearing wigs?"

Kirsty didn't reply. She was watching a pirate who had just sat down and started to pull off his boot.

"There's something funny about them," she murmured.

At that moment, the pirate's foot popped out of his boot. The girls instantly knew what was funny about the pirates.

"They're goblins!" Rachel exclaimed.

The goblin pirate rubbed his large, green foot and winced.

"What are they doing on board the *Rainbow Pearl*?" asked Kirsty in dismay.

"Look, there's the captain," said Rachel.

Even with his pirate hat and blue frock coat, Rachel and Kirsty recognised Jack

Frost at once.

"We have to find Padma," said Kirsty. "Something has gone terribly wrong."

"I'm here," said a miserable voice.

The girls whirled around and saw Padma sitting in the *Golden Galleon*'s mizzenmast rigging.

"Padma, what happened?" cried Rachel.

"Jack Frost and his scurvy goblin pirates ambushed me in the night and made me walk the plank," said Padma. "He wants to be a world-famous pirate – bigger than Blackbeard. The ship grew to

human size as soon as Jack Frost was in command. Now he has all my magical treasures, and I have no fairy magic at all."

"None?" Rachel asked in alarm.

"All my power comes from the magical objects I told you about yesterday," said Padma. "Without them, I can't even get back to Fairyland. The magic of pirates everywhere will be ruined, and the festival and all the visitors will be in danger."

"We want to help," said Kirsty at once. "Jack Frost isn't going to get away with this. We'll get your treasures back and recapture the *Rainbow Pearl*."

A flicker of hope appeared in Padma's brown eyes.

"With your help, I know I'll get my

ship back," she said.

"Look, the crew is leaving," said
Rachel.

A long line of pirate goblins was
stomping down the gangplank.

"Come back when your pockets
are stuffed with treasure," Jack Frost

yelled after them.

"Aye aye, Captain Frostbeard," the pirate goblins squawked.

Two pirate goblins stayed on the ship, guarding the top of the gangplank.

"How are we going to sneak past them?" asked Kirsty.

Padma leapt down from the rigging and tucked herself into Kirsty's neckerchief.

"Let's see if we can find something to distract the goblins so we can get on board," she said.

Chapter Four
Cannon-Fire

Mr and Mrs Tate said that the girls could go and explore, so they hurried down the *Golden Galleon*'s gangplank to the harbourside. There was already a crowd of visitors and pirates, and music and sea shanties filled the air. There were higgledy-piggledy stalls offering carved

toys, pirate outfits, maps and sizzling
street food. A small group of pirates was
standing around a cannon, getting ready
to put on a display.

Rachel and Kirsty weaved through the
crowd, getting closer to the *Rainbow Pearl*.
Then a group of pirate goblins swaggered
past, and the girls darted out of sight
behind a dressing-up stall.

"They're absolutely dripping with
jewels," said Rachel in astonishment.

The pirate goblins were half hidden
under ropes of pearls and dangling
earrings. Tiaras were piled on their
heads, and their arms were sparkling
with bracelets. As they passed a red-
headed pirate queen, her crown slipped
off her head and landed in a pirate
goblin's hands. He cackled with glee and

balanced the crown on top of his tiaras.

"How has this happened?" asked Kirsty.

"It's because Jack Frost has my bejewelled treasure chest," Padma explained. "Its power is drawing all the booty to the pirate goblins like a magnet."

Just then, the man who was running

the dressing-up stall started to put the costumes away.

"Are you closing already?" Rachel asked.

"I can't sell these costumes," the man grumbled. "They're supposed to come with earrings and bags of treasure, but I can't find them anywhere."

"Please don't leave yet," said Rachel. The girls hurried away.

"We have to stop Jack Frost before he spoils the festival," said Kirsty.

Suddenly, Rachel had an idea. She pulled Kirsty back through the crowd to where the cannon was standing.

"Look," she said, pointing at the sign in front of it. "The display starts at half past nine. Maybe a loud noise will distract the pirate goblins for long enough to let us get on board."

"How are we going to take the ship from Jack Frost and two goblins?" asked Kirsty.

"We don't have to," said Padma. "We just need my magical objects. Each one will give me back some of my power. When I have all three, the *Rainbow Pearl* will be mine again."

At twenty-nine minutes past nine, the girls crouched down beside the *Rainbow Pearl*'s gangplank.

"We'll have to move quickly," Kirsty whispered. "This is our only chance."

They watched the pirates load the

cannon and light the fuse.

BOOM! The noise was deafening. The pirate goblins on deck squawked and fell down, hiding their heads.

"Now!" cried Padma.

Rachel and Kirsty sprinted up the gangplank, and then dived across the deck and down the ladder into the belly of the ship. After the bright sunshine, the inside of the ship looked dingy. The only

light came from the faint blue glow that the girls had seen before.

"Why is the ship glowing blue?" Kirsty asked.

"Because Jack Frost is in charge," said Padma. "The *Rainbow Pearl* doesn't like it. Let's head towards my cabin. That's where I keep my treasures."

The girls tiptoed along the corridor.

Every creak made their hearts thump
faster. If just one pirate goblin heard
them, their mission would be ruined.
They picked their way through store
rooms and sleeping quarters. Hammocks
were half pulled off the walls and the
floor was littered with dirty clothes. What
a mess the goblins had made!

At last they reached the dark, panelled door of the captain's cabin. Kirsty pushed open the door and gasped. There was Jack Frost, bending over a jewel-studded treasure chest.

Chapter Five
The Pirate Code

Jack Frost spun around and saw them.

"How did you get on board?" he said with a snarl. "Guards!"

They heard the thunder of pirate boots racing across the deck above.

"You'll walk the plank for coming aboard without the permission of

Frostbeard the Fearsome," Jack Frost went on.

The girls exchanged a confused glance.

"Who?' asked Rachel.

"Me!" he yelled.

"We're here to take back Padma's things," said Kirsty in a firm voice. "We're not going to walk any planks."

"This treasure chest is mine now," Jack Frost retorted. "Pirates steal things. That's what we do."

Cackling with laughter, he lifted the chest into a cupboard and slammed the door shut. Padma was still hidden in Kirsty's neckerchief.

"I just need to touch the chest to make it mine again," she whispered. "If only we could get that door open."

The gang of pirate goblins skidded

through the doorway.

"About time!" Jack Frost yelled. "What did you do, stop for forty winks on the way? Throw them off the ship!"

"Aye aye, Captain Frostbeard sir," the pirate goblins gabbled.

Rachel and Kirsty shared a worried look. How were they going to get out of this? Then Rachel remembered Padma's words. *I just need to touch the chest to make it mine again.* There was only one problem. The treasure chest was inside the cupboard, and Padma was too small to open it.

"One favour!" Rachel cried suddenly. "The pirate code says you have to grant prisoners one favour."

Jack Frost scowled at her.

"I haven't read the pirate code yet," he muttered. "Fine, have your silly favour."

"Let me have one more look at the treasure chest," said Rachel.

Kirsty glanced at her best friend, and Rachel flashed her a tiny smile. Kirsty smiled too.

"Get ready," she whispered to Padma.

"This is the last time you'll ever see it," Jack Frost said in a mean voice, opening the cupboard door.

Lightning fast, Padma darted out from Kirsty's neckerchief. The pirate goblins bounded across the cabin, but Padma was already at the cupboard door.

"Too late, scallywags," she declared.

She laid her hand on the treasure chest, and it instantly shrank to fairy size. Jack Frost let out a howl of rage.

"I think the blue glow faded a bit," cried Kirsty.

Padma nodded, beaming from ear to ear.

"A third of my powers just came flooding back to me," she said.

"No!" Jack Frost roared.

Padma waved her wand and the pirate goblins' jewellery vanished.

"My tiaras!" wailed the first.

"My earrings!" the second complained.
"My bracelets! My stick-on belly-button
diamond!"

"They've gone back
to their rightful owners,"
said Padma.

Jack Frost went purple
with rage.

"Your other magical
objects won't be so easy
to find," Jack Frost hissed.

He shoved the girls
aside and strode out of
the cabin. The group of
pirate goblins scurried after him.

"I'm going to take this chest to
Fairyland," said Padma. "I'll ask Queen
Titania to look after it."

"I'm glad you've got one of your

magical objects back," said Rachel.

"All thanks to you two," said Padma.
"I'll be back soon."

She disappeared in a puff of magical
sparkles. Rachel and Kirsty flashed each
other an excited smile.

"Let's head back to the *Golden Galleon*," said Kirsty. "This weekend is going to be even more amazing than we thought!"

Story Two
The Swashbuckling
Pirate Hat

Chapter Six
Goblin on the Galleon

The *Golden Galleon* was covered with
tiny, fluttering pirate flags from the
crow's nest to the bowsprit. Jake waved
to Rachel and Kirsty as they went back
on board. The girls saw several fierce-
looking pirates stomping around the ship.

"What's going on?" asked Kirsty.

"The *Golden Galleon* is hosting the start of the Pirate Olympics," Jake told them. "These rapscallions are the event organisers."

"I've never heard of the Pirate Olympics," said Rachel.

"I wonder if Olympia knows about them," Kirsty whispered, remembering their past adventures with the Games Fairy.

"The events are being held all around Briny-on-Sea," said Jake. "There's athletics, gymnastics, rowing, diving, sword-fighting . . ."

"It sounds amazing," said Kirsty. "What's the first event?"

"Gymnastics," said Jake with a grin. "The competitors have to swing high up in the rigging."

The pirate athletes were warming up
on the main deck, and the organisers
were checking that everything was ready.
There was even a pirate first-aid team,
dressed all in green.

"Look at the crowd on the
harbourside," said Kirsty. "Everyone's here
to watch the Pirate Olympics, and we've
got the best view of all."

As Jake went to check on the competitors, Rachel noticed one last flag rolled up on the poop deck.

"They missed one," she said. "Let's hang it up for them."

As the girls walked closer, the flag began to glow. Rachel and Kirsty dropped down beside it in excitement: they knew that magical glow. The flag unrolled and Padma tumbled out.

"Ahoy!" she said. "That's the strangest way I've ever boarded a ship."

She stood up and shook back her curly hair.

"It's great that you're here," said Kirsty. "They're just about to start the Pirate Olympics right here on the *Golden Galleon*."

Padma looked alarmed.

"Uh-oh," she said. "My swashbuckling pirate hat protects pirates from accidents, but it won't work while Jack Frost has it. With events like hook throwing and sword-fighting, all sorts of horrid accidents

could happen."

"Thank goodness there's a first-aid team here," said Kirsty. "Rachel, we have to find that hat!"

BOOM! A shockingly loud cannon blast made them all jump.

"Hide under my hair," said Rachel to Padma. "I think the first event is about to start."

"Welcome, me hearties, to this year's Pirate Olympics," boomed the chief organiser. "The first event, the rigging gymnastics, tests strength, skill and style. Good luck, everyone!"

The pirate gymnasts lined up, and Kirsty nudged Rachel.

"The pirate on the end is much shorter than the others," she said. "Do you think he could be a goblin?"

"His feet do look very big," said Rachel. "I bet you're right, and that he's got Padma's hat to keep him safe."

"This is our chance to get it back and save pirates from being injured," said Kirsty.

The girls ran over and pulled on the goblin's arm.

"We know why you're here," said Kirsty

as he swung around. "You – oh!"

The pirate was a young boy.

"I'm here to compete," he said, looking confused.

"Good luck in the competition," gabbled Rachel, feeling her cheeks going red. "Sorry."

The girls stumbled backwards and bumped into the organisers.

"Watch out," said one.

"Steady," said another.

One of them let out a high-pitched giggle. Kirsty glanced at him and gasped. He was one of the pirates from the *Rainbow Pearl*, and he was wearing a glowing pirate hat.

Chapter Seven
Risky Rigging

"You have to give that back," Kirsty exclaimed.

"Leave me alone, pesky humans," the pirate goblin hissed.

They tried to block his way, but he scuttled away from them.

"We found it!" Rachel whispered.

It was wonderful to know that Padma's second magical object was so close. But how were they going to get it back?

There was a second cannon boom, and the competition began. People whooped and cheered as the pirates swarmed up the rigging. Then the quickest competitor got his boots tangled in the ropes. He tugged hard, lost his grip and fell backwards, dangling upside down from the rigging. The crowd gasped, but the pirate goblin howled with laughter.

"You look like a fly in a spider's web," he screeched at the poor pirate.

The second competitor was reaching out for the crow's nest when a gust of wind rocked the ship. The pirate fell – the spectators screamed – but luckily she landed in the fishing net that was

stretched out below.

"My heart is pounding," Kirsty
exclaimed.

The young boy was the only pirate left
in the competition now. He climbed the
ropes slowly and steadily.

"That's it, lad, take care," roared the organiser from the deck.

But then ... *RRRIP!* The rigging sagged, and the boy was flung against the mast. With a cry, he let go of the rope and plunged into the water. *SPLASH!* A groan went up from the crowd.

"Ha ha!" the pirate goblin crowed. "This isn't the diving event, stupid!"

The boy climbed back on board, dripping wet, and there was a feeble round of applause from the harbourside. The organisers shook their heads at each other.

"This hasn't been a great start to the Pirate Olympics," said Rachel. "And we know why."

"They're moving on to the next event," Padma whispered. "We have to get closer to the goblin."

But the pirate goblin was already walking over to the ship's plank with the other organisers.

"It's time for the diving," announced the chief organiser. "We'll be looking out for grace and flair. Today we have two pirate queens and a pirate king competing for the title."

Kirsty looked at the pirates in their magnificent costumes.

"They're going to dive in their clothes," she said. "Oh dear. I have a horrible feeling that this is going to be a right royal disaster."

There was a drum roll,

and the first pirate queen walked to the end of the plank. She held up her arms, leapt into the air . . . and did a massive belly flop into the water. The pirate goblin cackled with laughter.

"Is she OK?" cried Rachel, leaning over the side of the ship.

The pirate queen was already climbing up the side of the ship. She climbed back on to the deck and rubbed her tummy.

"Ouch," she said. "Oh well, better luck next time."

"Pirates are meant to sail, not swim," called out the pirate goblin in a mocking

voice.

The pirate queen glared at him and went to be checked by the first-aid team. The drum rolled again, and this time a pirate king walked to the end of the plank. He looked impressive at first. But was he as tall and strong as he seemed?

Chapter Eight
A Right Royal Disaster

"His legs are shaking," said Padma. "Uh-oh."

The pirate king sank to his knees and hugged the end of the plank.

"I've gone all dizzy," he called out. "My knees hurt."

The organisers hurried forwards and

helped the pirate king back on to the ship. The pirate goblin screeched with laughter.

"Useless!" he cackled.

He wasn't looking at the girls. Rachel tiptoed up behind him. Maybe she could lift the hat off his head before he turned and saw her . . .

But the pirate goblin looked over his shoulder and scowled at her.

"Leave me alone," he hissed. "Jack Frost is going to be a world-famous pirate, and you can't stop us."

"Oh yes we can," Kirsty muttered.

"As long as he has

my hat, pirates will keep having silly accidents," said Padma with a sigh. "People will stop dressing up as pirates, and then Jack Frost will be the only one left."

"We won't let that happen," Kirsty promised.

Just then, the drum roll sounded again.

"Oh dear," said Rachel. "The third diver hasn't had her turn."

The pirate queen strode out to the end of the plank. She raised her arms above her head, bent her knees and jumped. *CRACK!* The wooden plank snapped and she fell into the water in a tangle of arms and legs. The crowd groaned.

"I feel so helpless without my magic," said Padma.

Kirsty noticed another three pirates

climbing down the side of the ship. The goblin was leaning over the wooden railing and mocking them.

"The next event is bound to go wrong too," said Kirsty with a groan. "Can't we stop them?"

"Too late," said Rachel. "Look, they're already getting into the rowing boats."

"Good luck," roared the chief organiser. "Heave HO!"

The starting cannon boomed, and the rowers pulled on their oars. Two boats shot forwards, and one shot backwards.

"Wrong way!" shouted the crowd.

"The pontoon's over there, dopey!" shouted the pirate goblin, leaning out over the rail.

"Turn around," Rachel called out.

Everyone cheered as the boat turned

around . . . and then groaned as it headed towards the rocks. The chief organiser clapped his hands over his eyes.

"The others are having trouble too," said Padma.

The pirate in the second boat pulled
on his oars and fell backwards head over
heels. The third pirate yanked her oars
too roughly and hit herself on the head
with them.

"Ouch!" she yelled, clutching her head
and dropping an oar into the water.

The pirate goblin was laughing so hard
that tears were running down his face.

He leaned even further over the rails,
and then disaster struck. The magical hat
slipped off his knobbly head and dropped
into the water.

"No!" he shouted.

"No!" cried the girls.

"Fly down and get it," Rachel cried.

"I can't," Padma exclaimed. "Everyone would see me."

The hat was already floating away from the *Golden Galleon*, and a cheer went up as the three rowers seemed to get a little better and headed for the shore.

"My hat!" wailed the goblin. "My hat!"

But at that moment, the second rower scooped the hat out of the water on his oar. He threw it as hard as he could towards the *Golden Galleon*.

Chapter Nine
Wingless

Rachel and Kirsty leapt up, but the goblin elbowed them aside and snatched the soggy hat out of the air.

"Mine," he snapped, jamming it back on his head.

At that moment, another cheer went up. The second of the pirate rowers had

won the race.

"Right, me hearties," said the chief organiser. "Time for pirate athletics – hopefully we'll have a bit more success on dry land!"

"The athletics will be a disaster too, unless we get that hat back," said Padma. "Let's follow them."

Everyone followed the organisers towards Briny-on-Sea's cobbled high street. Even though Rachel and Kirsty were worried about the hat, they couldn't help but smile when they saw the merry little town centre. Pirate flags fluttered from every shop, and a live band was singing sea shanties, with visitors dancing in the street. Brightly coloured stalls were offering craft lessons, face-painting and glitter tattoos.

Many of the visitors were dressed up, and the crowds bristled with pretend cutlasses and fake beards. There were even a few real parrots squawking among the pirates, and signs advertised a mermaid show, a floating museum and a best-dressed pirate competition.

There was so much to see that for
a moment the girls forgot what they
were doing. Then the voice of the chief
organiser boomed out.

"Make way, make way," he bellowed.

Everyone moved to the side, and the
girls saw that a rough obstacle course
had been laid out.

"Starting at this end of the street, our
pirate athletes must hurdle the treasure
chests," announced the chief organiser.
"After that they'll throw the hook and
toss the peg leg, then sprint to the other
end. Give them all a cheer!"

It was a terrible performance. Three
of the pirates fell over the hurdles and
scraped their knees. Four more flung their
hooks so high that they got stuck on the
roofs. Two others bonked each other on

the head while throwing their peg legs, and the last one twisted her ankle while she was hobbling to the finish line. The first-aid team almost ran out of plasters and bandages.

"At this rate, no one will win a medal!" the chief organiser muttered.

Kirsty took Rachel's hand and pulled her behind a face-painting stall.

"Padma, can you turn us into fairies?" asked Kirsty. "We have to do something to stop this."

The Pirate Fairy waved her wand, but there was only a faint glimmer of fairy dust.

"My magic is too weak," Padma said with a groan. "I'm sorry, but until I get another magical object back, I'm not strong enough to turn you into fairies."

"Then we'll just have to get the hat back as humans," said Kirsty.

Rachel and Kirsty came out from behind the face-painting stall and stopped, shocked. The organisers and the goblin had completely disappeared, and the crowd was moving off.

"Where are we going?" Rachel asked a teenage girl.

"It's the sword-fighting next," said the girl. "My favourite."

"Oh my goodness, this could be dangerous," said Rachel in alarm.

The girls ducked and weaved through the crowd, and caught up with the

organisers in the town square. The sword-
fighters were already choosing their
weapons, and the goblin was rubbing his

hands together with glee.

Just then, someone in the crowd sneezed.

"That gives me an idea," said Kirsty.

Chapter Ten
Winged Pirates

"If we could make the goblin sneeze hard enough, maybe his hat would fall off," Kirsty said.

"It's worth a try," said Padma. "You just need something that will tickle his nose . . ."

A large seagull nearby tilted its head

on one side as if it had heard the little
fairy. Then it ruffled its wings and a large
feather dropped to the ground.

"Wow, that was lucky," said Rachel.

"It's almost as if—"
She broke off in
astonishment as
the seagull gave
them a little
wink and flew
away.

"The seagulls are
my friends," said Padma.
"They often fly along beside the *Rainbow
Pearl.*"

Kirsty reached out and gently tickled
the tip of the pirate goblin's long nose
with the feather.

"Ahh-choo! Ahh-CHOO!"

Shaken by sneezes, the goblin's eyes
streamed, but one hand held his hat
firmly in place.

"It's no use," said Kirsty. "He's not
letting go."

Just then, a little girl nearby gave a
loud squeal.

"My chip!" she wailed. "That seagull took my chip."

"What a bold bird," said a lady nearby. "It swooped down and snatched the food right out of her hand."

"A pirate seagull," said another lady with a chuckle.

Rachel gave a sudden gasp.

"I've got an idea," she said in an excited voice. "Padma, you said that the seagulls are your friends. Do you think they'd use their chip-stealing skills to help you?"

They hurried over to the seagulls. Rachel found a rather squashed biscuit in her pocket and held it out to the birds. As the seagulls flocked around, Padma peeped out from under Rachel's hair.

"Ahoy, me hearties," she said. "Will you

help a fellow pirate?"

She explained what had happened, and the seagulls squawked loudly. Then they rose up in a flapping mass of grey and white wings, shrieking.

"Oh my goodness," said Kirsty, putting her hands over her ears. "They're louder than twenty goblins."

The seagulls dived low over the crowd, and everyone ducked. But the birds were only after one thing. They made a beeline for the goblin, who squealed as

he disappeared under
a mass of feathers
and beaks. Seconds
later, the seagulls
rose into the air in
a tight group. They
swooped back across
the crowd, making
everyone duck again,
and then dropped the
hat at Rachel and
Kirsty's feet.

"Yes!" Rachel
exclaimed. "Thank
you, seagulls!"

The girls dropped
to their knees so that
the hat was hidden
between them. Then

Padma slid down Rachel's hair, just like a pirate sliding down the rigging. As soon as she touched the hat, it returned to fairy size.

BOOM! The starting cannon sounded.

"Just in the nick of time," said Kirsty, smiling at her best friend. "Phew!"

"I can feel my magic surging back into me," said Padma. "Soon I'll be able to take back the *Rainbow Pearl* from those scurvy scallywags with a click of my fingers. Thank you both for all your help."

"Are you going to take the hat to

Fairyland for safekeeping?" Rachel asked.

"Yes," said Padma. "But I'll soon be back to raise the fairy flag above the *Rainbow Pearl*. Hurray!"

Story Three
The Jolly Parrot

Chapter Eleven
Silly Shanties

The sea-shanty band stomped their feet and roared out their song.

"What shall we do with the grumpy farmer?
Sing her a song and don't alarm her.
Feeding the chickens just might calm her,
Don't forget the tractor!"

Rachel and Kirsty exchanged a

confused look.

"Those aren't the right words," said Rachel.

Other people seemed confused too. The band looked wonderful, standing on a stage that was made to look like a ship. They had rich singing voices. But they couldn't seem to remember a single word of their songs.

"Let's go and look at the stalls," said Kirsty, tugging on Rachel's arm.

They had spent all morning exploring the festival, from the pirate museum to the best-dressed pirate competition. They had watched a skirmish on the beach and learned how to tie five different types of knot. They were excited about the pirate parade that afternoon. But they hadn't seen Padma or a single goblin.

"Look at this," said Rachel, stopping at a little stall that was garlanded with shells. "They're giving away treasure maps."

A handful of scrolls were sitting in a silver tankard, each tied with a colourful ribbon. Kirsty picked up a tightly rolled parchment with a purple ribbon.

"Goodness, it's heavy," she said.

"And it's glowing," said Rachel in excitement. "Quickly, Kirsty, let's find a hiding place where we can open it."

Behind a stripy sweet stall, the girls untied the ribbon and unrolled the scroll. Instead of a map, they saw a picture of Padma, drawn in ink.

"It's moving," Kirsty said with a gasp.

The lines of the picture flowed as Padma raised her hand and waved. Then the parchment flooded with colour, and Padma pulled herself out of the paper and winked at them.

"How did you do that?" asked Kirsty in astonishment.

"Pirate skills," Padma said, smiling.

"Have you come back to find your final magical object?" asked Kirsty.

"Yes, the jolly parrot," said Padma. "It helps people on board ship to communicate well. Now Jack Frost has it, things are

getting more and more confusing. Even pirates on dry land are finding it hard to understand each other."

Just then, the sea-shanty band started to play the tune of 'My Bonnie Lies Over the Ocean'. The music was beautiful, but everything went wrong when they started to sing.

"*My mummy has gone to the café,*
My mummy is sipping her tea.
My mummy has ordered a sandwich,
O bring back my mummy to me."

Some people in the crowd started to giggle. There was a loud twang as several guitar strings snapped, and the singers glared at each other.

"The musicians all think that the others in the band are singing the wrong words," said Padma with a sigh. "This will make them quarrel."

"We must find that jolly parrot," said Rachel. "Padma, have you got enough magic to turn us into fairies? It would be easier to see goblins in the crowd if we could fly overhead."

"Let's find out," said Padma.

She swished her wand in a zigzag pattern. Like a burst of tiny golden

fireworks, the fairy dust covered Rachel and Kirsty in shining sparkles. Instantly, they started to spin on the spot.

Chapter Twelve
Goblins and Mermaids

With each turn, Rachel and Kirsty became smaller and smaller. In a few seconds they were both the same size as Padma, and they all shared a hug.

"Oh, I'm so happy to be a fairy again," said Kirsty, fluttering her gauzy wings. "Being able to fly is the best feeling in

the world."

Holding hands, the three fairies rose into the air, soaring over the crowds of pirates and holidaymakers.

"There's a parrot," cried Rachel, pointing at a blue-winged macaw sitting on a pirate queen's shoulder. "And another . . . and a cockatoo over there!"

"I see one too," said Kirsty, as a crimson parakeet squawked up at her. "Goodness, he sounds exactly like a goblin."

Padma burst into peals of laughter.

"Silly me, I forgot to tell you what to search for," she said. "The jolly parrot isn't a real parrot. It's my lucky emblem. It's made of silver, and I usually carry it in my pocket wherever I go."

"But that could be hidden anywhere," said Rachel. "In a drawer in Jack Frost's cabin, in a goblin's pocket . . . how are we going to find it?"

"We need a clue to tell us where to start looking," said Kirsty.

"AVAST!" screeched a loud voice from below. "Catch the mermaid and lock her in the brig!"

Shocked, the three fairies zoomed

towards the noise. A crowd had gathered
in front of a wooden stage, and Padma
perched on a lamppost above them.
Rachel and Kirsty landed beside her.

"It's a show," said Padma.

"Not just any show," said Kirsty. "Those
pirates are goblins in disguise."

Two goblins were prancing across the
stage in pirate costumes, and each had
a toy parrot on his shoulder. There was
a large tank in the middle of the stage,
and inside was another goblin. This one
was wearing a long, blonde wig, an
emerald-green bikini top and a glittering
mermaid tail.

"I look like the bee's knees," he crowed,
waving to the crowd. "Look at me! Look
at how amazing I am."

The crowd laughed and clapped.

"Stop showing off," snapped the tallest goblin pirate. "Get on with the play."

"Throw the nets around the mermaid!" bellowed the other goblin pirate. "Catch her and we will sell her to the king."

"BOOO!" cried the audience, enjoying themselves hugely.

"The goblins aren't having any trouble communicating with the audience," said Rachel. "Do you think they might have the jolly parrot?"

"Let's find out," said Kirsty.

She swooped down towards the stage and scooted out of sight behind the tank,

followed by Rachel and Padma. Kirsty stopped so suddenly that the others bumped into her.

"Look out," she said. "It's Jack Frost!"

Jack Frost was dressed as an elegant pirate king. Padma gasped and pointed at the polished wooden

cane in his hand. A silver parrot was set into the top, and Padma's eyes sparkled with happiness.

"That's my jolly parrot," she said.

Jack Frost turned on his heel and strode away from the stage. The fairies fluttered after him as he headed towards the main street.

"Quickly, under his coat tails," whispered Padma. "We have to hide before he gets out in the open!"

Chapter Thirteen
Jack Frost's Plan

The fairies swooped under Jack Frost's long, swishy coat and held on tight. Seconds later, they were being swept through crowds of pirates and visitors.

"Listen," said Rachel. "He's talking."

"That doesn't sound like him," said Kirsty.

"Make way for the greatest pirate of all time," the Ice Lord was saying in a rich, booming voice. "I am the unforgettable Frostbeard the Fearsome. No one can stop me! Out of my way, tiresome humans!"

"Goodness me, he's certainly communicating what he wants," said Padma. "No one could misunderstand him."

"Clear a path, or walk the plank," Jack Frost roared.

Rachel peeped out from under the coat and saw people scuttling out of the way.

"He's heading towards the *Rainbow Pearl*," she said. "Oh look, it isn't glowing as blue as it was before."

"That's thanks to the swashbuckling pirate hat," said Padma. "When the jolly

parrot is back where it belongs, the ship
will be mine again."

Jack Frost stomped up the gangplank
and picked up a telescope from beside the
ship's wheel. He gazed out to sea through
it, and then gave an unpleasant little
laugh.

"Another ship full of pirates arguing, and all thanks to me," he said to himself. "Soon this will be the only pirate ship where everything goes like clockwork."

He stroked the jolly parrot's silvery head, and Padma gritted her teeth.

"That scoundrel," she whispered.

"They won't even make it in to harbour," said Jack Frost. "Nincompoops! Soon they'll all be begging to work on my ship."

He turned and strode towards the ladder that led to the captain's cabin. Rachel, Kirsty and Padma slipped out from under his coat and fluttered up to the crow's nest. Perching on the edge, it was easy to see a pirate ship on the horizon.

"That must be the ship that he was

talking about," said Rachel.

"Without the jolly parrot, the pirates on that ship won't be able to communicate," said Padma. "There will be misunderstandings and arguments, and they won't be able to steer her into the harbour."

"Let's help them," Kirsty said.

The fairies glided down from the crow's nest and soared over the churning blue-green waves. Smiling dolphins and

whiskery seals popped out of the water to call to them as they sped along.

"Ahoy, maties!" called Padma, waving to them.

"We can't stop," Rachel sang out. "We have to help that ship."

As soon as they reached the vessel, they saw that things had gone badly wrong. The captain was clutching his hair, the sails were flapping loose and every single pirate was shouting.

"I said climb the mizzenmast!"

"No, you said climb the mainmast!"

"To port!"

"No, to starboard!"

"Haul on the rope!"

"Not that one!"

"Secure the main sail!"

"No, I said lower the top sail!"

"This is terrible," said Padma. "They're not listening to each other. If they don't start working as a crew, they'll scuttle the ship."

"Can't you use your magic to help them?" Rachel asked.

"Not with the jolly parrot working for Jack Frost," said Padma. "Oh dear, I don't

know what to do."

"I have an idea," said Kirsty. "But we have to fly back the way we came – quickly!"

Chapter Fourteen
Seals and Dolphins

Kirsty zoomed off and Rachel and Padma flew close behind her. Soon they saw the seals and dolphins playing in the water ahead.

"I bet they could help to get the ship to shore," Kirsty said to Padma.

The fairies hovered just above the

water, and soon the dolphins and seals were crowding around them. Padma tapped one dolphin and one seal with her wand, and they sparkled with fairy dust.

"Now they will be able to understand us," she said.

She told the animals about Jack Frost stealing her magical objects, and how the jolly parrot was confusing the pirates.

"We'll help," said the dolphin in a musical voice. "We can swim beside the ship and guide it in the right direction."

"We can nudge it along too," said the seal, whose voice was gruff and kind. "Don't worry about the pirates, Padma, we'll get them safely home."

Feeling excited, Rachel, Kirsty and Padma flew to the bowsprit. They sat with their legs dangling down and

watched as the dolphins and seals
gathered around the ship. Then, with the
tiniest of jolts, the ship began to turn.

"What's going on?" the captain
shouted.

Spray was flung into the air and the
ship started moving towards the shore.
The pirates cheered as they went faster
and faster.

"Great work, seals!" called Padma,

leaning over the bowsprit.

"Well done, dolphins!" Kirsty exclaimed.

As the ship reached the harbour, Rachel spotted Jack Frost glaring at them from on board the *Rainbow Pearl*.

"Look, he's shaking his fist," said Kirsty.

The fairies waved goodbye to the seals and dolphins.

"The ship is safe," said Rachel. "Let's go and get the jolly parrot back."

Everyone was watching the seals and dolphins leave. They didn't notice three tiny fairies flutter over to the *Rainbow Pearl*. Jack Frost glared at them as they perched on the railing.

"You spoiled my fun," he said in a cold hiss. "Get off my ship."

"It's Padma's ship," said Kirsty. "Please be kind and give back the jolly parrot."

"Why should I?" Jack Frost asked.

"Because you're enjoying this festival as much as anyone," exclaimed Rachel. "You don't want it to be spoiled, do you?"

"I don't mind if it's spoiled for everyone else," said Jack Frost, shrugging. "As long as I'm having a good time, who cares about the humans?"

Just then, the Briny-on-Sea church clock bonged.

"We're running out of time," said Padma. "The pirate parade is about to start. Without the jolly parrot, the festival organisers won't be able to communicate and the parade will be a disaster."

Jack Frost laughed and twirled his cane across his fingers.

"He looks like a majorette twirling a baton," said Rachel.

"What's a majorette?" demanded Jack Frost.

Suddenly, an idea popped into Rachel's head.

"Maybe that's the answer," she whispered.

"What do you mean?" asked Kirsty.

"Let's try to make him throw the

cane up in the air like a baton," Rachel replied. "One of us might be able to catch it."

Chapter Fifteen
Shimmer and Shake

"What's a majorette?" Jack Frost yelled again. "Answer me!"

Padma waved her wand, and for a moment twenty fairy-sized majorettes in gold-trimmed uniforms were marching across the deck, twirling batons and shaking pom-poms. Then, in a twinkle of

fairy dust, they had disappeared.

"Those are majorettes," said Padma. "They do performances with their batons, just like you twirling your cane."

"Of course, they're very skilful and fast," said Kirsty.

"I can go fast," said Jack Frost.

He sped up and the cane wobbled across his hand, but he didn't drop it.

"They can throw their batons up in the air and catch them, still twirling," added Rachel.

"I can do that," said Jack Frost at once. "Easy peasy, lemon squeezy."

He flung the cane upwards . . .

"Now!" cried Rachel.

Padma zoomed up, her hands outstretched.

"Stop her!" Jack Frost roared.

"Yo ho ho!'
A pirate goblin
swung out from
the rigging and
caught the cane. He
laughed at Padma's
disappointed face.

"You pesky fairies
aren't quick enough
to beat me," he
boasted, spinning
the cane around.
"I'm the most
amazing pirate
ever."

Padma buried
her face in her
hands, but Rachel
and Kirsty were

watching the cane. The goblin spun it faster . . . faster . . . and dropped it!

"No!" Jack Frost yelled as the cane fell.

It landed with a loud *CRACK*. Something broke off and spun across the deck – something small and silver.

"The jolly parrot!" all three fairies exclaimed.

Padma and Jack Frost dived for the parrot. But Rachel and Kirsty fluttered their wings in front of Jack Frost's face, and he couldn't see where he was going.

"Yes!" cried Padma as she scooped up her last magical object.

The jolly parrot returned to fairy size as soon as she touched it. Padma rose up to hover in front of Jack Frost, and then clicked her fingers.

"Nincompoop!" Jack Frost was yelling,

shaking his fist at the pirate goblin. "You've scuppered my chance to rule the seas and I'm – wait! What's happening?"

The last trace of a blue glow had left the *Rainbow Pearl*, and it started to shimmer and shake.

"This is a fairy ship," said Padma. "It's about to go back to its normal size."

"You should probably leave," Kirsty added.

"Abandon ship!" Jack Frost yelled.

He jumped on to the plank and took a flying leap into the water. The pirate goblin was close behind him. Seconds later, the ship shrank to fairy size and rose out of the water.

"Oh my goodness," said Rachel. "What if someone saw that happen?"

"Don't worry, there is no one here," said Padma, winking at her. "They are all watching the pirate parade – and that's exactly where we should be."

She sailed her ship over Jack Frost and the goblin, who were pulling themselves on to the harbourside, dripping wet. Padma flicked her wand, and their clothes were dry again. Jack Frost shook his fist at the *Rainbow Pearl*.

"I have a feeling that I will be seeing Frostbeard again one day," said Padma.

"We'll be ready to help," Kirsty promised her.

"It's almost time for me to make you human again," said Padma. "But first . . ."

The enchanted ship sailed through the

air, leaving a sparkling trail of fairy dust
in its wake. In Briny-on-Sea's main street,
the sound of laughter and sea shanties
filled the air. Padma tapped the ropes
with her wand, and the ship turned and

hovered above the main festival float. Then it started to sink downwards.

"They'll see us," said Rachel with a gasp.

"Yes," said Padma, laughing. "But people will think that we're just a toy ship, and part of the parade."

The fairies ducked out of sight as a cheer went up from the crowd. The *Rainbow Pearl* landed at the front of the float, above the pirate king and queen. Tingling with excitement, Rachel and Kirsty peeped out at the people waving flags, banners and cutlasses. None of them knew that they had just seen real magic!

"The festival has been saved and the parade is a success," said Padma. "Thank you so much, Rachel and Kirsty."

"We loved helping you," said Kirsty.

"Being pirates is fun," Rachel agreed.
"This has definitely been our most
swashbuckling adventure ever!"

The End

Now it's time for Kirsty and
Rachel to help ...

Rita the
Rollerskating Fairy

Read on for a sneak peek ...

"I love the Cool Kids Leisure Centre,"
said Kirsty Tate.

She held out her arms and twirled
around in the middle of the foyer.

"Me too," said her best friend, Rachel
Walker. "I'm so glad it opened halfway
between Tippington and Wetherbury. It's
brilliant that we get to choose an after-
school club together."

Lucy, the lady who was organising the
after-school sports clubs, looked up as
they walked over to her.

"How was the bike club?" she asked.

"It was even more exciting than we expected," said Kirsty, sharing a secret smile with Rachel.

With the help of Bonnie the Bike-Riding Fairy, Rachel and Kirsty had chased a cycling goblin around the countryside, ridden a raft down a rushing river and rescued Bonnie's magical bracelet. As friends of Fairyland, they were used to enchanted adventures. But their adventure with Bonnie had been one of the most exciting yet.

"I'm very glad to hear that you had fun at the bike club," said Lucy. "There are two other clubs running this afternoon. Would you like to try rollerskating next?"

"That would be great," said Rachel. "I love rollerskating."

"The teacher, Liz, has set up in hall two," said Lucy. "She'll fit you with a pair of rollerskates each."

Rachel and Kirsty thanked her and hurried towards hall two. They opened the door and met a blast of pop music and laughter. Rollerskaters were skidding slowly across the room.

Read Rita the Rollerskating Fairy to find out what adventures are in store for Kirsty and Rachel!

Read the brand-new series
from Daisy Meadows...

Ride. Dream. Believe.

Meet best friends Aisha and Emily
and journey to the secret world of
Unicorn Valley!

Calling all parents, carers and teachers!
The Rainbow Magic fairies are here to help
your child enter the magical world of reading.
Whatever reading stage they are at, there's
a Rainbow Magic book for everyone!
Here is Lydia the Reading Fairy's guide to
supporting your child's journey at all levels.

Starting Out

Our Rainbow Magic Beginner Readers are perfect for first-time readers who are just beginning to develop reading skills and confidence. Approved by teachers, they contain a full range of educational levelling, as well as lively full-colour illustrations.

Developing Readers

Rainbow Magic Early Readers contain longer stories and wider vocabulary for building stamina and growing confidence. These are adaptations of our most popular Rainbow Magic stories, specially developed for younger readers in conjunction with an Early Years reading consultant, with full-colour illustrations.

Going Solo

The Rainbow Magic chapter books – a mixture of series and one-off specials – contain accessible writing to encourage your child to venture into reading independently. These highly collectible and much-loved magical stories inspire a love of reading to last a lifetime.

www.rainbowmagicbooks.co.uk

"Rainbow Magic got my daughter reading chapter books. Great sparkly covers, cute fairies and traditional stories full of magic that she found impossible to put down" - Mother of Edie (6 years)

"Florence LOVES the Rainbow Magic books. She really enjoys reading now" - Mother of Florence (6 years)

Read along the Reading Rainbow!

Well done – you have completed the book!

This book was worth 2 stars.

See how far you have climbed on the Reading Rainbow opposite.
The more books you read, the more stars you can colour in
and the closer you will be to becoming a Royal Fairy!

Do you want to print your own Reading Rainbow?

1) Go to the Rainbow Magic website

2) Download and print out the poster

3) Colour in a star for every book you finish
and climb the Reading Rainbow

4) For every step up the rainbow,
you can download your very own certificate

There's all this and lots more at
rainbowmagicbooks.co.uk

You'll find activities, stories, a special newsletter
AND you can search for the fairy with your name!